Phoebe Gilman

Jillian Jiggs

Scholastic Canada Ltd.

Toronto New York London Auckland Sydney
Mexico City New Delhi Hong Kong Buenos Aires

The Jillian Jiggs books:

Jillian Jiggs
The Wonderful Pigs of Jillian Jiggs
Jillian Jiggs to the Rescue
Jillian Jiggs and the Secret Surprise
Jillian Jiggs and the Great Big Snow

The illustrations for this book were created in gouache on Arches watercolour paper.
The type was set in 16 point American Typewriter.

Scholastic Canada Ltd.
175 Hillmount Road, Markham, Ontario L6C 1Z7, Canada

Scholastic Inc.
555 Broadway, New York, NY 10012, USA

Scholastic Australia Pty Limited
PO Box 579, Gosford, NSW 2250, Australia

Scholastic New Zealand Limited
Private Bag 94407, Greenmount, Auckland, New Zealand

Scholastic Ltd.
Villiers House, Clarendon Avenue, Leamington Spa,
Warwickshire CV32 5PR, UK

National Library of Canada Cataloguing in Publication

Gilman, Phoebe, 1940-2002.
Jillian Jiggs / Phoebe Gilman.

ISBN 0-439-96185-8

I. Title.

PS8563.I54J5 2004   jC813'.54
C2004-901754-3

6 5 4 3 2   Printed in Canada   05 06 07 08

A long time ago, when she was quite small,
Jillian Jiggs wore nothing at all.

"Those were the days," her mother would sigh,
As she looked round the room and started to cry.
For Jillian Jiggs liked to dress up and play,
And this made a mess in her room every day.

"Jillian, Jillian, Jillian Jiggs!
It looks like your room has been lived in by pigs!"
"Later. I promise. As soon as I'm through,
I'll clean up my room. I promise. I do."

Now, Jillian meant every word that she said,
But later the promise flew out of her head.
When Rachel and Peter started to shout,
Jillian had to, just had to go out.

"Oh, look at the boxes! Yippee! Hooray!
It's hard to believe someone threw these away.
I'm mad about boxes. Boxes are fun.
No one will guess who we are when we're done."

No one would guess...

But a mother would know.
A mother could tell by the tip of a toe.

"Jillian, Jillian, Jillian Jiggs!
It looks like your room has been lived in by pigs."
"Later. I promise. As soon as I'm through,
I'll clean up my room. I promise. I do."

"We'll help, Mrs. Jiggs. We'll do it. Don't worry.
We'll all work together. We'll clean in a hurry."
They started to clean up her room, it is true.
They started to clean, but before they were through...

Jillian thought up a game that was new.
They had to stop cleaning. What else could they do?
"Let's dress up as pirates. Tie sails to the bed.
Heave ho, you landlubbers! Full speed ahead!"

They dressed up as dragons.

They dressed up as trees.

They dressed up as bad guys who never say please.

They dressed up as chickens, cooped up and caged.

They turned into monsters who hollered and raged.

They cackled like witches. They stirred and they boiled.

Then they were royalty, pampered and spoiled.

They tiptoed and twirled like little light fairies.

They made themselves wings and flew like canaries.

Whenever they thought that was it, they were through...

She'd change all their costumes and start something new.

Then Jillian's mother came in with her mop,
Took one look around and...

...fainted, KERPLOP!

"Jillian, Jillian, Jillian Jiggs!
It looks like your room has been lived in by pigs!"
"Later. I promise. As soon as I'm..."

"Start cleaning this minute, this second, not later!
I want this room tidy. I want this room straighter!"

"You'd better go now, Rachel and Peter.
See you tomorrow when everything's neater